Magic Animal Friends

For Ann Dymond,
remembering evenings with Jaime

Special thanks to Valerie Wilding

ORCHARD BOOKS

First published in Great Britain in 2014 by The Watts Publishing Group

5

A CIP catalogue record for this book is available from the British Library.

ISBN 978 1 40834 844 4

Printed and bound in Great Britain
by Clays Ltd, Elcograf S.p.A.

The paper and board used in this book are made from wood from responsible sources

FSC www.fsc.org
MIX
Paper from responsible sources
FSC® C104740

Orchard Books
An imprint of Hachette Children's Group
Part of The Watts Publishing Group Limited
Carmelite House, 50 Victoria Embankment, London EC4Y 0DZ

An Hachette UK Company

www.hachette.co.uk
www.hachettechildrens.co.uk

Ellie Featherbill All Alone

Daisy Meadows

ORCHARD

Shining House
Sunshine Meadow
Blossom Briar
Goldie's Grotto
Toadstool Cafe
Toadstool Glade
Mrs Taptree's Library
Library
Friendship Tree
Maze
Silver Spring
Buttercup Gro
Lighthouse

Map of Friendship Forest

Can you keep a secret? I thought you could!
Then I'll tell you about an enchanted wood.
It lies through the door in the old oak tree,
Let's go there now - just follow me!
We'll find adventure that never ends,
And meet the Magic Animal Friends!

Love
Goldie the Cat

Contents

CHAPTER ONE

Friends in the Forest

"*Peep! Peep!*"

"Dad," Lily Hart called, "the ducklings are hungry!"

"Give them some seeds to keep them happy," her dad said, clearing the work table where he treated poorly animals. "I'll check them over in a moment."

Lily's best friend, Jess, grabbed some seeds from a bag. "I love helping your parents," she told Lily. "I'm so glad we're best friends."

Lily grinned at Jess. Her parents ran the Helping Paw Wildlife Hospital in a converted barn behind their cottage in Brightley village. Both girls loved working in the hospital, or feeding different creatures in their pens outside.

Soon the ducklings had gobbled up the all the seeds.

"Come on, greedy," said Mr Hart, lifting one of them onto his table.

"What will happen to them now?" asked Jess.

"If Dad says they're strong enough, we'll release them back where we found them on Brightley Stream," Lily explained. "The poor things had been abandoned by their mother.

They were all alone and very hungry."

"Feathers – fine. Feet and bill – excellent. Weight – perfect," said Mr Hart, popping the duckling into a box. "Next?"

Lily carefully passed him another duckling, while Jess picked up a third.

"Its feathers are so soft," Jess said, cuddling the little bird against her jumper. "Will they be able to find food for themselves?"

"Easily!" said Lily. "They've lived on our pond for the last few days, eating duckweed, grass, worms, slugs…"

"Yuck!" said Jess. She pretended to

shudder, making her blonde hair swing.

Mr Hart laughed. "It might be yuck to you," he said, "but it's not yuck to a duck!" He placed the last duckling into the box. "Ready to go!"

"Can we release them?" Lily asked.

"Please?" begged Jess.

"Of course," said Mr Hart. He lifted the box into Jess's arms. "You carry them, and Lily will show you exactly where we found the little things. Have fun!"

They set off for Brightley Stream. Jess walked very carefully, keeping the box level. They could hear the ducklings scrabbling around inside it.

"Dad doesn't need to worry about us having fun," said Lily with a smile. "Especially with Goldie around!"

Goldie the cat came from Friendship Forest, a magical world filled with talking animals. She had already taken Lily and Jess on two adventures there.

Each time, Lily and Jess had helped stop Grizelda, an evil witch, from driving the animals away.

"I hope we see Goldie soon," said Jess.

Lily nodded. "She said she'd find us if Grizelda was up to no good again."

The girls gently set the ducklings on the water near the stepping stones.

"They look happy!" Jess said.

The ducklings bobbed around, dipping their beaks in the stream, but always staying close together. Gradually they grew braver, and one climbed the bank to peck the grass.

When Lily stood to brush off her tunic, she felt something soft touch her leg. She looked down, expecting to see a duckling, but saw instead a beautiful cat with golden fur and eyes as green as fresh lettuce.

"Goldie!" she cried in delight. "She's back!"

The girls stroked the purring cat. Goldie rubbed around their ankles, then mewed up at them and darted towards the stepping stones that crossed Brightley Stream. She looked back at the girls and they knew exactly why she wanted them to follow her.

"She's taking us to Friendship Forest!" said Jess with a grin. "Come on!"

They followed Goldie across the stream and through Brightley Meadow to the Friendship Tree. It looked like a huge, dead-looking oak tree, but as the golden cat ran up to it it burst into life. Fresh green leaves and scented blossoms sprouted from the branches.

The girls had seen this before, but they still couldn't help gasping at the sight.

Goldie reached up a paw to where letters were carved into the tree trunk. The girls knew that they must read the words aloud.

Holding hands, Lily and Jess said, "Friendship Forest!"

A little door, just as tall as their shoulders, appeared in the trunk. Jess reached for the leaf-shaped handle and opened it. A shimmering, golden light poured out of the tree.

The cat slipped through the door and

Jess and Lily ducked their heads, following her into the golden glow. Their skin tingled all over, and they knew that they were becoming a little smaller.

As the light faded, they were thrilled to find themselves once more in a sun-dappled forest clearing, surrounded by trees and flowers.

"Toadstool Glade!" said Lily. "It's so beautiful."

"And magical," Jess breathed.

Nestling amongst the nearby trees were pretty little cottages, where the animals of Friendship Forest lived.

"Welcome," said a soft voice. They turned to see Goldie. She was now standing upright, as tall as the girls' shoulders, and wearing a golden scarf.

Jess and Lily hugged her and, as they did so, other creatures appeared, rushing to greet them.

"Hello! I'm Bertie," a young badger as high as the girls' knees told them. "I heard that you saved the Treasure Tree from the Boggits!"

The Boggits were Grizelda's horrible, filthy, smelly servants, who did everything she told them to do. They had already

tried to destroy the beautiful Blossom Briar and the Treasure Tree that gave the animals their food.

"Nice to meet you, Bertie!" said Jess, shaking the paw he stretched up to her. She whispered to Lily, "I know we've been here before, but isn't it still amazing to talk to the animals?"

Before Lily could reply, the girls heard a squeak and looked down to see a pretty little mouse.

"Molly Twinkletail!" Lily said, kneeling down.

Molly was holding a carefully wrapped present that was twice as big as she was.

"Is someone having a birthday?" asked Jess.

"Yes, Ellie Featherbill, the duckling," said Molly. "We're all going to her party later. Come on, Bertie, let's go and wrap your present for Ellie."

They rushed off, calling, "See you soon!"

Lily turned to Goldie. "Have you brought us here to help again?" she asked. "Jess and I wondered if Grizelda was up to something."

Their cat friend looked serious. "She might be," Goldie said. "The butterflies say that something strange is happening by Willowtree River. They're not sure what."

Jess grinned. "Then let's find out. Come on!"

CHAPTER TWO

Flippershells to the Rescue

Jess and Lily hurried through the forest after Goldie. Soon they caught a glimpse of sunlight glinting on silvery water.

"That's Willowtree River," Goldie said.

"It seems so calm," said Lily. "I wonder why the butterflies thought something strange was happening."

She tried to look more closely at the river, but her view was blocked by one of the beautiful willow trees. Some stepping stones led out to the centre of the river and Lily ran across them, stopping on a large one in the middle. Jess and Goldie followed and stood beside her.

"Can you see anything?" asked Jess.

Lily shook her head. The sparkling water looked clean and peaceful.

Just then, an orb of yellow-green light appeared over the water. Lily's tummy fluttered. They'd seen that light before!

It zoomed towards them, then with a flash and a *cra-ack*, the orb exploded into green sparks. In its place on one of the stepping stones stood a tall, thin woman, wearing a shiny purple tunic and trousers, and high-heeled boots with sharply pointed toes.

"Grizelda!" cried Lily.

The witch glared. Her long green hair twisted about her head like a nest of snakes. The air around the girls seemed to turn cold.

"Silly girls!" she sneered. "And the foolish cat! You won't spoil my plans this time. When my Boggits have finished, the forest will be ruined. No more trees and flowers!" She laughed, her eyes flashing. "Green is for hair, not leaves!"

Jess clenched her fists. "We won't let you ruin Friendship Forest," she said, trying not to let her voice tremble.

Grizelda cackled. Then her hair sparked and she began muttering.

"What's she doing?" Lily

asked nervously.

Goldie swallowed. "I think she's casting a spell."

"Oh no! Look at the river!" cried Jess.

The water swirled, turning sludgy brown as it churned up mud from the bottom. It rose higher and higher until it lapped at their toes. In no time, the river had covered over all of the stepping stones except the one they were standing on!

"Now what do we do?" cried Lily.

"Stop interfering, that's what!" Grizelda screeched. "You can't stop me. When my Boggits are finished, all the animals will have to leave – and I can have Friendship Forest for myself! Ha!"

Snapping her fingers, she disappeared in a yellow flash.

"Thank goodness she's gone," said Lily. "But now we're trapped!"

Goldie gave a groan. "And while we're stuck here, we can't stop the Boggits from carrying out her plan. I wonder what she's told them to do this time?"

Jess was peering into the water. "Do you think we could wade to the bank?"

Lily picked up a stone. "I'll throw this in. If we can see it land, it'll be shallow enough to paddle across."

She tossed the stone.

Plop!

It sank out of sight.

"The water's still swirling," said Jess, "but maybe we could swim…"

"I can't swim at all," said Goldie. "Oh, what are we going to do?"

As they stood thinking, Jess spotted something moving in the water. It looked like a large, round flat stone. "What's that?" she cried. "A swimming stone?"

"Look! There are six more following behind," said Lily.

As they watched, something bright red bobbed up in front of the first swimming stone, then bobbed down again.

Goldie clapped her paws. "That's not a stone, it's a turtle!" she said. "It's the Flippershell family." She splashed the water with her paw. "They'll hear that," she explained.

The red blob bobbed up again.

Jess and Lily grinned when they

realised it was indeed a turtle's head – wearing a swimming hat!

"Ahoy there, Goldie!" the turtle called.

Six more heads popped up, each wearing a brightly coloured hat.

Goldie explained what had happened. "Can you help us get to shore?" she asked.

"Aye, aye," said the biggest turtle. "Flippershells! Stepping stones from the island to the bank," he ordered. "Rainbow formation! Go!"

The turtles swam into line. Each called out their hat colour as they reached their position.

"Red!" That was the big turtle.

"Orange!"

"Yellow!"

"Green!"

"Blue!"

"Indi – indi – go!" puffed a little one.

The last turtle was swimming in circles, singing quietly to herself. The others sighed, "Come on, Violet!"

Once they were in line, Mr Flippershell

called, "Rainbow formation, ready and waiting?"

"Aye aye, sir," they replied.

"Hold fast!" Mr Flippershell ordered. They clasped flippers. "Go, Goldie!"

Jess and Lily followed the cat, hopping across the turtles' backs to the river bank. They all shouted their thanks to the Flippershells.

"One last thing," said the big turtle. "If you go upriver, watch out. Those horrible Boggits were heading that way. Making trouble, I'll be bound."

"I bet he's right," said Goldie as they hurried along the water's edge. "They must be carrying out Grizelda's orders."

Soon they came in sight of a pretty blue barge moored against the riverbank. It had a yellow cabin on the deck, and round, yellow portholes just above the waterline.

"That belongs to the Featherbill family," said Goldie. "They take care of

Willowtree River. They're probably inside, getting ready for Ellie's birthday party."

Suddenly, the barge rocked violently from side to side.

"That's weird," said Jess. "Little ducks couldn't make it rock like that."

"I know who could," Goldie said grimly. "Boggits! They must be onboard!"

CHAPTER THREE

Boggits on the Barge

The barge rocked harder, churning the water into frothing waves.

"It's going to tip over!" Lily cried.

But just as the barge looked like it really was about to capsize, they saw the Boggits clambering onto the roof of the cabin. They were snorting and yelling.

"Hide!" hissed Goldie, pulling the girls down behind a cluster of bulrushes. "Oh, I hope the Featherbills are okay!"

Jess parted the bulrushes to take a look. "The Boggits are reaching into the cabin through the portholes," she whispered. "They're pulling things out and throwing stuff in the river. It's sandwiches!" she said in surprise. "And cakes and – woah! There goes a bowl of jelly!"

"That must be for Ellie's party," said Lily. "They're spoiling it!"

Four scruffy Boggits laughed as they hurled food over the side of the barge.

Their fur, made up of patches of dingy green, washed-out blue and sickly yellow, was matted with mud, and their rotting-cauliflower smell wafted downriver to Goldie and the girls.

"Chuck it in the water!" yelled Pongo, tossing a pie overboard.

"Hegga hegga!" Whiffy chuckled.

"Mucking up the river!"

"Boggits make Grizelda happy," shouted Reek.

Lily and Goldie gasped as Sniff heaved the birthday cake into the water, shouting, "Eat up, fishes! Boggits hope you be sick!"

Jess had seen enough. She stood up, shouting, "Stop! Stop now!"

The Boggits spun around and caught sight of her and the others.

"Girls!" roared Pongo. "Boggits don't like you!" He grabbed a loaf of cherry bread and flung it at Jess.

She dodged it and yelled, "What have

you done with the Featherbills?"

As soon as she spoke, there were loud squawks and flaps as the whole Featherbill family came flying out from another clump of bulrushes further downstream.

They landed in a flurry of feathers on the riverbank next to Lily and Jess. Lily counted seven ducklings, besides their mum and dad.

"We were too scared to come out until we saw you," said Mr Featherbill as the ducklings huddled around their mother's legs.

Mrs Featherbill was close to tears. "What a flapdoodle! Those Boggits have ruined Ellie's party, and just look what they're doing to our river." She wiped her eyes with a wingtip. "If they carry on like this, they'll pollute it so badly that our fish friends will have nowhere to live. Nor will any of the river creatures."

The girls and Goldie shared a worried glance. "So that must be Grizelda's plan," Jess said. "She wants to spoil the river to drive away the animals!"

Lily kneeled to comfort Mrs Featherbill. "We've come to help," she said. "We won't let the Boggits win."

"One, two, three…" said Mr Featherbill, counting his ducklings. "No… One, two… Keep still, children. One, two, three, four…"

"Don't worry," said Lily. "I counted them as they landed. There are seven."

"Seven?" cried Mrs Featherbill. "There should be eight! Who's missing?" She waddled around the ducklings. "There's Lulu and Dilly, Stanley and Rodney," she said. "Keep still, children. There's Betty, Bobo and Sunny. Oh, no! Where's Ellie?"

Lily gasped. "She must still be on the barge!"

"Ellie hates noise," Mrs Featherbill said tearfully. "The Boggits must have frightened her so much she was afraid to come out."

Little Betty said, "She was hiding in the bucket on deck."

Everyone peered through the bulrushes.

"There!" said Betty. "See the bucket?"

Lily was puzzled. "Yes, but I can only see pink flowers peeping over the top."

"That's her birthday crown," sobbed Lulu.

Jess stroked the duckling's soft head. "Don't cry," she said gently. "Lily, Goldie and I will save Ellie. Come on, you two!"

Crouching, the three friends ran to the barge and pressed themselves against the side. But before they could decide what to do, Reek untied the mooring rope and the barge began to move!

Lily, Jess and Goldie watched in dismay as Pongo steered it away from the bank.

"Boggits find where the river begins," he grunted.

Reek and Sniff did a stomping dance, making the barge rock wildly again.

Whiffy chuckled. "Hegga hegga. Boggits clever to steal ducks' boat. Now we can make river bad forever!"

Lily gasped. "Where are they going?"

Goldie put her paws to her mouth. "They must be going to the source of the river. If they spoil the water there, it will all flow downstream."

"But that means the whole river will be polluted!" cried Jess. "We've got to stop them."

Lily caught a last glimpse of little pink flowers poking out of the bucket.

"Oh, Jess," she said. "Poor Ellie must be terrified. We have to save her!"

CHAPTER FOUR

Silvia and her Sisters

Mr and Mrs Featherbill waddled over to the girls and Goldie.

"Oh, no! Ellie will be so frightened," Mrs Featherbill worried aloud.

"We'll go after the barge," Lily promised, "and bring her back safe and sound."

"And we'll stop the Boggits from polluting the river, too," said Jess.

Goldie smiled at the Featherbills. "These girls are brave and clever," she told them. "They'll keep their promises."

Jess got up. "Let's go."

Goldie and Lily followed her upriver. They could still see the barge, but they couldn't catch up with it because the bank was covered with flowers, reeds and prickly brambles. Soon, the plants and bushes became so dense that they couldn't go any further.

"The barge is completely out of sight

now," said Jess. "What are we going to do?"

Lily spotted something shining in the sun. It was on the river, but tucked into a thick clump of rushes. Then she saw a long curving neck.

"A swan!" she said. "But it can't be. It's silver. There's no such thing as a silver swan."

"Let's see," said Jess, pushing through the rushes. "Hey!" she called back. "It's a sort of swan – but come and look!"

Lily and Goldie joined her at the river's edge. Bobbing gently in the shallows was a silver painted raft. The front was shaped like a swan's neck and head. Three silver-speckled white ribbons trailed into the water, one from the graceful neck, and the others from the front corners.

"Why don't we use this to follow the barge?" suggested Jess. "Jump on."

Lily held back. "There aren't any oars," she said. "How can we make it go upstream?"

"You can't," said a clear, firm voice. "That raft belongs to me and my sisters."

They spun around to see three snow-white swans emerging from a group of shady trees. The front one wore a pretty sunhat, but she looked stern and very proud as she stared down her bill at them.

"Careful, girls," Goldie murmured. "Swans aren't always friendly."

"I know," whispered Lily. "We had one at the wildlife hospital once, and it chased me out of the pen when I tried to feed it, then banged on the gate with its hard beak!"

"I'll be careful," whispered Jess. She gave the swans a friendly grin. "Excuse me," she said. "We need to rescue a duckling, and we have to get upstream. Could you take us on your raft? Please?"

The swan sisters looked at each other. "What do you think, Silvia?" said one of the swans.

"We could, I suppose," the swan called Silvia replied. "But we would want something in return."

"Anything," Lily said.

Silvia explained that she'd lost her favourite necklace. "I came in for a steep landing," she said, "and my necklace fell off and landed in a tree. My wings are too wide to fly between the branches."

"Show us where the necklace is, Silvia," Lily said. "We'll get it back for you!"

The swan stretched her elegant neck towards a lime tree. Dangling from a high branch was a string of pearls.

Goldie grinned. "Easy!" she said. In seconds she was halfway up the tree, leaping from branch to branch. She stopped and called down, "I can't see it because of all the leaves."

"Left a bit," Lily called, guiding her.

“Up to the next branch – look right – there!”

With a flick of her paw Goldie freed the necklace, and down it tumbled into Lily’s cupped hands.

She put the necklace on Silvia. “There!”

The grateful swan ruffled her feathers in delight. “Thank you!” she said, then turned to her sisters. “Ladies, the raft!” she told them. “We have a duckling to rescue!”

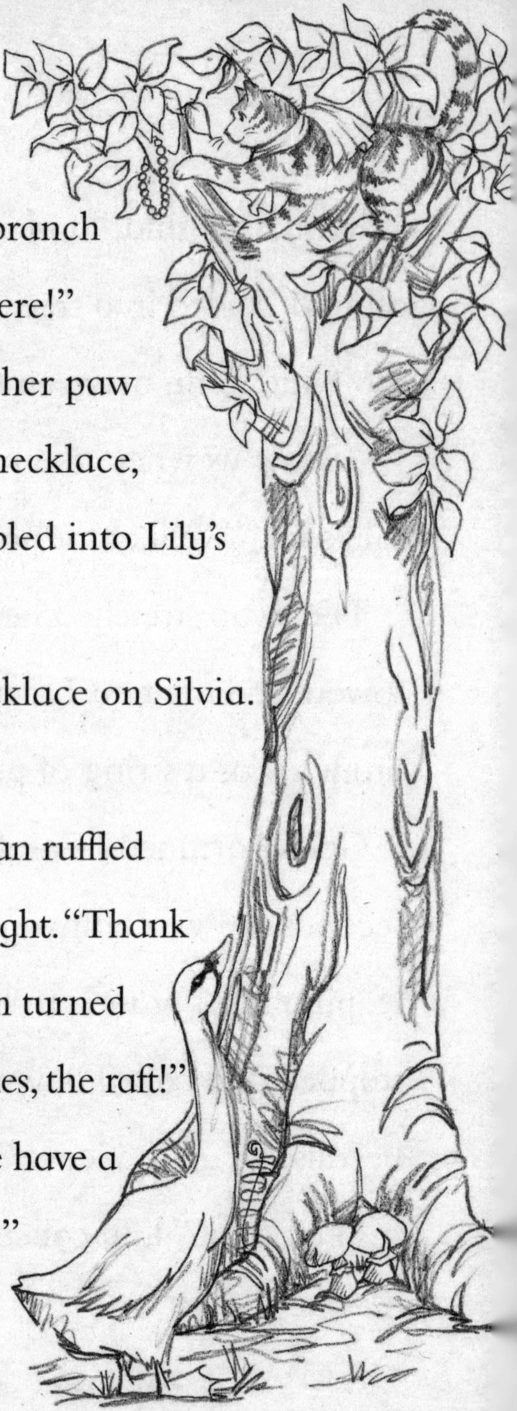

CHAPTER FIVE

Journey to the Island

Jess stepped carefully onto the raft, followed by Goldie and Lily.

Each swan took a silvery ribbon in her beak and started pulling the raft along.

The river was quiet apart from birdsong and the hum of insects. Lily trailed a hand in the water.

"This would be a lovely ride," she said, "if only we weren't so worried about Ellie and the Boggits."

Goldie pointed upstream to where the river forked. "We're almost there," she said.

"But which way?" asked Jess. "Left or right?"

"It doesn't matter," Goldie said. "The right side goes around an island and joins up with the left side. This is as far as the river goes."

Lily's eyes widened. "So the source must be on that island!" she said.

Goldie nodded. "It's hidden, right in the centre of Mystery Maze."

Jess and Lily exchanged a glance. Mystery Maze! That sounded fun!

The island was bordered by a high, thick hedge. The swans towed the raft towards the shore and they drifted along, curving around the bank until Jess gave a shout.

"The barge!" she cried. "It's moored up ahead."

Lily shaded her eyes from the sun. "It looks quiet," she said. "The Boggits are probably already in Mystery Maze, searching for the river's source."

"Come on," said Jess. "Let's get there first and stop them polluting it."

Goldie held her back. "What about Ellie?" she said. "She's probably hidden herself somewhere on board. Silvia," she called, "stop the raft beside the barge, please."

The swans pulled them silently through the water, until the raft bumped gently against the bank, right next to the barge.

Goldie, Jess and Lily jumped ashore, calling their thanks to the swans. Then they climbed carefully aboard the barge and began searching for Ellie. The

Boggits had messed it up so much during their journey up the river, it looked like a different boat. Furniture had been hauled out of the cabin and thrown around the deck. Squashed food and crumbs coated the roof and there were huge dirty footprints all over the place.

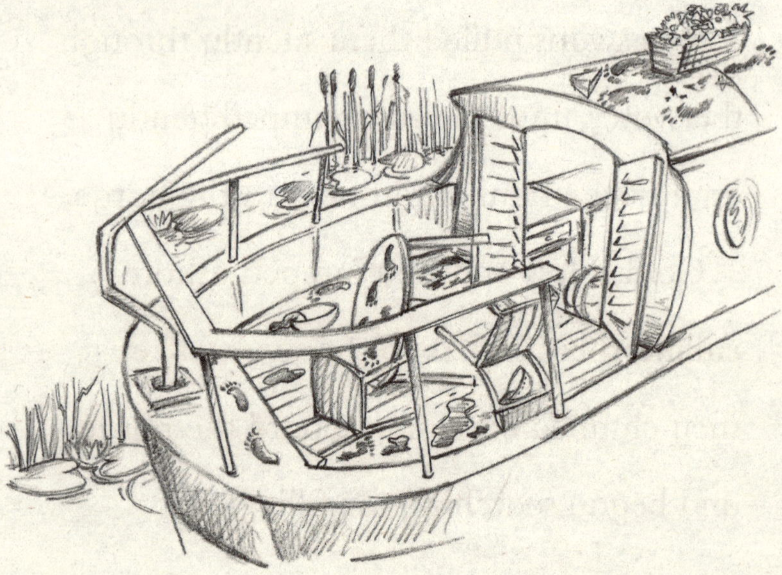

Lily made a face, stirring a pile of rubbish with the tip of her shoe. "What a disgusting mess those Boggits made!"

They searched for the duckling, calling softly, but she was nowhere to be seen.

"Poor Ellie! She must be so scared. And it's her birthday, too!" Goldie said sadly.

"Don't worry," said Lily, taking the cat's paw in her hand. "We'll do our best to make it up to her."

Jess jumped ashore again. "To do that, we've got to find her first," she said, turning left. "Let's try this way."

"You won't find Ellie over there," came

a small voice.

The girls and Goldie looked around but they couldn't see anybody.

"Who said that?" asked Lily.

"I did! Look down here!" called the little voice.

"Oh, it's Dotty Redcoat!" exclaimed Goldie, peering at a sunflower stalk. Sitting there was a little smiling red ladybird.

"Hello, Goldie," said Dotty.

"Hello, Dotty! These are my friends, Jess and Lily," said Goldie. "Did you say that you know where Ellie Featherbill is?"

"Yes, I do," said Dotty. "I saw her sneak away from the barge when the Boggits weren't looking. She went into the Mystery Maze."

Lily looked horrified. "How will a little duckling find her way around the maze? She might be lost in there forever!"

Goldie smiled. "She'll be fine," she said. "One of the Featherbills' duties is to check that the source of the river is clean and pure. Ellie will have been there many times. In fact," she went on, "she'll probably go straight there, thinking it's a safe place to hide from the Boggits."

"That's good," said Jess. "But suppose the Boggits sneak along behind her? She'll lead them straight to the source!"

"Then we'd better hurry. Thank you for your help, Dotty," said Goldie.

"You're welcome! I hope you find her," replied Dotty, before fluttering away.

The three friends entered Mystery Maze. Lily could feel her heart beating more quickly, and she and Jess shared a worried glance. Could they find their way through the maze before the Boggits? Goldie looked worried too, her tail twitching nervously from side to side.

"Let's look down here," she said, leading the girls through the hedges.

They moved quietly, trying to head towards the centre, but the high walls of hedgerow twisted and turned until they hadn't a clue which direction was which.

Soon they were completely lost!

Lily groaned as they reached yet another dead-end. "What are we going to do?" she asked. "No matter how hard we try, we're never going to find Ellie!"

CHAPTER SIX

"Bash them! Smash them!"

A stomping noise from the other side of the hedge made them stop still. It was followed by a snuffling sound.

"Boggits!" whispered Goldie. "They're quite close."

They crouched down and peeped

through a gap in the hedge. All they could see were four pairs of furry, grubby feet, with filthy toenails.

Sniff's voice reached them. "Bodda, bodda, bodda!" she said crossly.

"Boggits has been in the maze for ages," Whiffy whined. "Now Boggits is at another dead-end."

"Nasty hedges is in the way," they heard Pongo growl. "Boggits bash them down!"

"Good idea," said Reek. "Boggits find river source quicker, then make it dirty and smelly."

"Bash the bushes," said Whiffy. "Bash them! Smash them!"

"All fall down!" laughed Sniff. "Haargh! Haargh!"

Jess and Lily couldn't see what was happening, but they could certainly hear. The Boggits stamped, grunted, ripped and tore, and the branches cracked and thudded as they fell. The sounds faded as the Boggits thundered off in a different direction.

"We need help," said Lily. "What about asking Mr Cleverfeather, the owl? He's got so many brilliant inventions in his shed. Surely there's one that can help us find Ellie?"

"Good idea," said Jess, "except Mr Cleverfeather's shed is so far away from here. We could shout as loud as we liked and he wouldn't hear us."

"Actually, I can hear you cloud and dear," came a voice from above. "I mean,

loud and clear."

"Mr Cleverfeather!" the girls cried. The owl flew into view. He was wearing a harness with whirring blades fixed to the back.

Jess stared in amazement. "He's turned himself into a helicopter!"

Mr Cleverfeather zoomed towards them and hovered just above their heads. "I was flying above the cheese

– I mean, trees – when Dotty Redcoat flew up to me. She told me you might need help finding Ellie." He glanced around the maze. "The hedges are too close together for me to land, but fevver near!"

Lily laughed. "He means, 'Never fear!'"

"We're so pleased to see you!" Jess told the owl.

Mr Cleverfeather lowered something down to them on a rope. It had a round disc on the end of a long handle. Goldie reached up to guide it to the ground.

"It looks like a metal detector," said

Lily. "Wait, It's got something written on the handle." She turned it around and read, "Feather Finder."

They looked blankly at each other. Then Jess called up, "Mr Cleverfeather, what's it for?"

"Bush the putton – I mean push the button," said Mr Cleverfeather.

"It will pull you towards Ellie!"

"Wow!" said Lily.

"It's attracted to feathers," called the owl. "Baby birds are always getting lost, so I use it to find the pittle lickles."

Lily giggled. "I think you mean 'little pickles'," she said. "Thanks—"

Before she could finish, there was an especially loud crash behind them. Down came a whole chunk of hedge!

There, looking as surprised as Goldie and the girls, were the Boggits!

For a moment, nobody moved. Then Pongo grinned, showing big, dirty teeth.

"Boggits wondered what that owl was up to," he said in his rough voice. "Fly away, owl!" he bellowed up at Mr Cleverfeather. "Girls and cat won't spoil Grizelda's plan this time." He turned to the other Boggits and jerked his grubby, hairy head towards Jess and Lily.

"Get them!"

CHAPTER SEVEN

A Wild Chase

As the Boggits lunged for the friends, Jess switched the Feather Finder on. It lurched away, pulling her through Mystery Maze. Goldie and Lily tore after her – left, right, then left again.

They left the Boggits quarrelling behind them.

"Pongo tripped me up!" roared Reek. "Whiffy pushed Pongo!" bellowed Sniff. "Oof!"

"Yow!"

"Aaargh!"

Lily glanced back at the pile of squabbling Boggits, but they were already struggling to their feet.

"Faster, Goldie!" she yelled.

The Feather Finder zipped right, left, then straight on between tall hedges. It zigzagged around fallen bushes, with Jess hanging on and Lily and Goldie close behind.

But the Boggits were close behind, too!

Suddenly, Lily felt a big furry hand touch her shoulder. Pongo! And he stank!

She screamed and pushed him away, racing after Goldie and Jess. Just as she was sure they would be caught, the

Feather Finder lurched through a gap in the hedge. Jess skidded after it, then Lily and Goldie scrambled through after her.

"That hole's too small for the Boggits," Jess yelled over her shoulder as the Feather Finder pulled her along. "They're too wide."

She was right. Soon they heard Sniff wail. "I is stuck!"

"Get moving, Reek," growled Pongo.

"Can't!" snapped Reek. "Sniff's big bottom's in the way."

Whiffy roared, "Boggits push!"

Lily heard a beeping sound. "That's the

Feather Finder!" she said. "We must be getting near Ellie."

They followed Jess around a corner.

"Faster!" cried Lily. "I can hear the Boggits on the other side of the hedge!"

The Feather Finder beeped furiously. *Beep! Beep!*

"We're getting closer," said Goldie.

Just as the *beep beep* turned into *beepbeepbeepbeepbeep*, they burst through the hedge and found themselves in a sunlit grassy clearing! In the middle, a crystal clear spring of water bubbled up like a fountain. As the water fell, it flowed into small channels that entered the ground in all directions, like the points on a clock.

"The source!" panted Jess, leaning on the Feather Finder to get her breath back.

"And look!" cried Lily. "There's Ellie!"

The little duckling, her birthday crown now tattered, was paddling in the small pool formed by the gushing water, staring with wide, frightened eyes.

"Boggits!" she whimpered.

As Lily ran to comfort her, the Boggits ran into the clearing. Reek jumped about in excitement.

"Boggits found the source!" he shouted.

Whiffy, Sniff and Pongo lumbered round in a clumsy dance. "Now Boggits can spoil the nasty river!" they chanted.

Jess winked at Goldie. "Do as I say," she whispered. "Lily, look after Ellie." Then she said loudly, "Quick, Goldie. Let's get back to that pile of revolting rubbish we found. We mustn't let the Boggits get it. They could use it to ruin the river!"

She and Goldie raced away.

The Boggits chased them, whooping with delight.

"Silly girl told us about lovely rubbish!" shrieked Whiffy.

"Haargh! Haargh!" laughed Pongo. "Boggits dump it in the river. Turn it nice sludgy brown!"

"Boggits make Grizelda happy!" puffed Reek, as they disappeared around a corner.

Lily picked Ellie up and smoothed the trembling duckling's feathers. "You're safe now," she told her.

Ellie wriggled against her. "I was so scared," she said in a shaky voice. "And the beautiful birthday crown my brother and sisters made for me is all ruined."

Lily kissed the top of her downy head. "Don't worry, Ellie. We'll make you a new crown, just as pretty as the first."

There was a hoot from above. "Hoo yoo!"

Lily looked up, grinning. Mr Cleverfeather even got "Yoo hoo" wrong!

"Ellie, can you remember how to get out?" the owl called down.

Ellie nodded. "Yes!" She hopped to the ground in a flutter of feathers. "It's this way, Lily. I'll show you."

Once Jess and Goldie were out of sight of the Boggits, they dived beneath a hedge and hid.

The Boggits stomped past.

Jess squeezed Goldie's paw. "We've tricked them," she whispered gleefully.

There was an angry bellow of "Girls gone!"

Then Reek growled, "Boggits found the source. Now Boggits lost it. Boggits can't make it dirty."

"Grizelda will be angry," Whiffy snarled. "Her plan not work."

Sniff's voice screeched, "Pongo's fault!" and an almighty squabble broke out.

"Let's go," whispered Goldie.

Jess heard a whirring sound and looked up to see Mr Cleverfeather hovering above them. She waved to catch his attention.

"Follow me!" he hooted. "I'll guide you out of the maze."

As Goldie and Jess crept away, they heard a rough, frightened voice. "Sniff doesn't want to be here when night comes. Might be monsters."

"Only hedges, no monsters," said Pongo.

But Jess didn't think he sounded too sure.

On and on they went, until at last they reached the exit, where Lily was waiting with Ellie in her arms.

"Listen," said Lily. "You can just hear the Boggits. They're panicking."

"Help!" Reek yelled from deep inside the maze. "Help! Boggits is lost!"

"Whiffy wants mud pool by Grizelda's tower!"

"Help!"

Mr Cleverfeather offered to go back and lead them out. "I think they've forgotten about Grizelda's plan by now," he chuckled, lowering the rope for his Feather Finder.

Lily tied it on. "Thanks for your help," she said.

"You were great!" said Jess.

"Mr Cleverfeather," said Goldie, "lead the Boggits away from the source, won't you?"

"I will, fevver near," he said, and flew off, leaving everyone giggling.

They headed back to the barge.

"We can get off the island," Lily said, "but what about the Boggits? We can't leave them here."

"Let them swim," said Jess.

"But they hate clean water," said Goldie. "They'll never get in."

A firm, clear voice said, "They will with our beaks behind them."

"Silvia!" cried Jess as the swan bobbed into view.

"We heard the shouting, so we stayed in case you needed help," said Silvia. "My sisters and I will see to the Boggits. You take the barge."

Lily smiled at the little duckling, nestled in her arms. "You'll soon be back with your family," she said.

"Oh, thank you!" said Ellie happily, and promptly fell asleep.

CHAPTER EIGHT

Roses and Cupcakes!

The river current soon carried the barge back to its usual mooring place. As they drew near there was a flurry of flapping wings and a lot of excited quacking.

Mr and Mrs Featherbill were thrilled to have Ellie back. Her brothers and sisters waddled happily around her and nuzzled her with their bills.

"Tell us about your adventure," they begged.

Ellie's parents thanked the girls and Goldie for saving Willowtree River. "I don't know what we'd have done if Grizelda's plan had succeeded," said Mrs Featherbill. "But thank you most of all for rescuing Ellie." She gave them each a warm feathery hug.

Mr Featherbill held out his wingtip to shake hands, but changed his mind and had a big hug, too.

"Now," said his wife, "there's still time for Ellie to have a birthday party, so let's get the barge ready for some fun!"

Lily, Jess and Goldie helped clean up and prepare the food, and Mr Featherbill flew off to tell all Ellie's friends there would be a party after all. When they'd finished tidying up, Lily and Jess slipped away and found a beautiful rose bush in a meadow. Together, they made a new flowery birthday crown, which they took back to the barge and placed on Ellie's head.

"Thank you, Lily and Jess!" Ellie said happily.

It wasn't long before everyone was sitting at a big table on the river bank next to the barge. Lots of Ellie's animal friends had arrived. Bertie the badger was there and Molly Twinkletail – and Mr Cleverfeather, of course.

The Flippershell family turned up in rainbow formation and floated on their backs in the river, with teacups balanced on their tummies.

Suddenly, there was a loud knock on the side of the barge. They looked over the edge to see Silvia and her sisters knocking with their strong beaks.

"Welcome to my party!" cried Ellie.

When everyone was full of honeybuns, hazelnut and cranberry cookies, mushroom patties and minty lemon fizz, Mrs Featherbill brought out a tray of birthday cupcakes. Each was topped with rosebuds made of creamy icing.

"I decorated the cupcakes myself," Ellie whispered shyly to Jess and Lily. "I'm glad the Boggits didn't find them." She touched each of the girls with a soft wingtip. "Thank you for saving me," she said, "and for keeping the river safe!"

"You're very welcome," Lily told her. "Happy birthday, Ellie!"

Soon it was time to go. Jess and Lily said goodbye to everyone and followed Goldie back through the forest to the magical tree with golden leaves. The cat touched a paw to the trunk and a door appeared.

"Grizelda will be angry that her plan failed," she told the girls. "She's sure to come up with a new way to try to make all the animals leave."

"Come and find us when she does," said Jess. "We'll do our best to stop her!"

Goldie hugged them both goodbye. Lily opened the door in the tree and the girls stepped into the shimmering golden light. When the glow faded, they found themselves once more in Brightley Meadow.

"Wow," said Jess, rubbing her eyes. "A barge of ducks, the Mystery Maze and a Feather Finder… That was an amazing adventure!"

They ran to the stream and giggled as

they skipped across the stepping stones, thinking of the Flippershells.

A little further along, they saw Jess's dad kneeling on the bank, feeding cake crumbs to the baby ducklings.

"Hello, you two," he said. "Lily's dad told me these little fellows had just been released, so I thought I'd bring them a treat." He laughed. "It's like a ducks' tea party!"

The girls grinned at each other. They knew what a ducks' tea party was really like!

The End

Grizelda is still trying to ruin the fun in Friendship Forest, starting with Goldie's sleepover! Lily and Jess have to help little kitten Bella in the next adventure,

Bella Tabbypaw in Trouble

Turn over for a sneak peek . . .

Jess used a stick to scrape her trainer clean and Goldie shook glistening water droplets from her fur.

"Now what?" Lily said. "We can't go any further, because of the swamp."

"The Boggits and Bella can't have come this way either. Let's go back to where we last saw footprints," Jess suggested.

It had stopped raining, but they had to splash through lots of puddles on their way back to where the prints had been.

"I definitely saw a print here," said Jess, stopping.

Tiggywinkles

Worlds Leading Wildlife Hospital

Lily's parents aren't the only ones who run a wildlife hospital.

Have you heard of Tiggywinkles – the world's busiest wildlife hospital? They take care of over 10,000 poorly animals every year and treat all kinds of wildlife, including hedgehogs, badgers, birds, foxes and deer.

If you are worried about a wild animal, you can have a look at their website for hints and tips about what to do.

www.tiggywinkles.com

Orchard Books supports Tiggywinkles.

Registered Charity No. 286447 Tiggywinkles,
Aston Road, Haddenham, Aylesbury,
Buckinghamshire HP17 8AF UK
Tel: 01844 292292
Email: mail@sttiggywinkles.org.uk

The path split into three directions. One led to the swamp and another went back to the Toadstool Glade.

Goldie pointed down the third path. "Bella must have gone that way – and those awful Boggits too. Come on!"

Read

Bella Tabbypaw in Trouble

to find out what happens next!

Magic Animal Friends

Read all the Magic Animal Friends adventures and be part of the secret!

Series One

COMING SOON!

Look out for
Jess and Lily's
newest adventure –
with adorable puppy
Poppy Muddlepup!

3 stories in 1!

www.magicanimalfriends.com

Puzzle Fun!

The mean Boggits have frightened poor Ellie Featherbill and now she's lost in the maze! Can you help her find the way out?

Lily and Jess's Animal Care Tips

Lily and Jess love helping lots of different animals – both in Friendship Forest and in the real world.

Here are their top tips for looking after...

DUCKS

like Ellie Featherbill

- Feeding the ducks at your local park is great fun! Lots of people feed them bread but this can be bad for them. Did you know ducks also like corn and lettuce as well as bread?

- Ducks like to live in clean water but there are lots of people who drop their litter in the park. Help keep their environment clean and clear by taking your rubbish home with you.

- If you have a dog make sure that you keep him or her on a lead so they don't scare the ducks swimming nearby.

- If you are concerned about a poorly-looking duck, ring your local wildlife animal hosptal for advice.

Magic Animal Friends

Can you keep the secret?

There's lots of fun for everyone at www.magicanimalfriends.com

Play games and explore the secret world of Friendship Forest, where animals can talk!

Join the Magic Animal Friends Club!

- Get special gifts
- Exclusive content
- All the latest Magic Animal Friends news!

To join the Club, simply collect all four tokens from the books in series one and send them in to us.

Don't forget to:
1) Include your name and address
2) Include the signature of a parent or guardian

Send your tokens to:
Magic Animal Friends Membership Offer,
Orchard Books Marketing Department
338 Euston Road, London, NW1 3BH

Terms and Conditions
(1) Open to UK and Republic of Ireland residents only (2) Purchase c Magic Animal Friends books is necessary (3) Please get the signature of your parent/guardian to enter this offer (4) The correct number of tokens must be included for the offer to be redeemed (5) Photocopie tokens will not be accepted (6) Membership packs are distributed on first come, first served basis whilst stocks last (7) No part of the offer is exchangeable for cash or any other offer (8) Please allow 28 days delivery (9) We may use your data to contact you with further membership offers (10) Prizes may vary from pictures shown. We reserve the right to offer prizes of an alternative or greater value.